Back-to-School Rules

by Laurie Friedman

Illustrated by
Teresa Murfin

CAROLRHODA BOOKS   MINNEAPOLIS

For Becca and Adam.
All my love, Mommy
—L.B.F.

For Tom, Serena & Phil
—T.M.

Carolrhoda Books
A division of Lerner Publishing Group, Inc.
241 First Avenue North
Minneapolis, MN 55401 U.S.A.

Website address: www.lernerbooks.com

Library of Congress Cataloging-in-Publication Data

Friedman, Laurie B., 1964—
    Back-to-school rules / by Laurie Friedman ; illustrated by Teresa Murfin.
      p.   cm.
    Summary: Wearing his monogrammed school cardigan, young Percy Isaac Gifford
explains his rules of success for getting the most out of the school year.
    ISBN: 978-0-7613-6070-4 (lib. bdg. : alk. paper)
    [1. Stories in rhyme. 2. Schools—Fiction. 3. Behavior—Fiction. 4. Etiquette—Fiction.]
I. Murfin, Teresa, ill. II. Title.
PZ8.3.F9116Bac 2011
[E]—dc22   2010003637

Manufactured in the United States of America
1 — PP — 7/15/11

I'm Percy Isaac Gifford.

Today's **an important** day.

You shouldn't frown or fret.
I'll tell you what you need to know.
When it comes to higher learning,
Stick with me. I'm a pro.

I get the most out of my school year.
I promise, you can too.
The rules of success are simple:
Just know what **NOT** to do.

The first rule you should follow:
Do NOT show up late!
You will be marked *tardy*.
Teachers do not like to wait.

Do not make excuses.
Don't blame everyone you know.
Don't say you were on time.
It was your family that was slow.

Another rule I live by:
DON'T BE IMPOLITE.
An apple a day won't work
If you don't know wrong from right.

Rule 2:
An apple a
day does not
keep the
teacher away.

That means no naps in class.
No running through the halls.
No climbing up the flagpole.
No writing on the walls.

No hiding school supplies
Or gobbling all the snacks.
Nothing in your teacher's seat:
No gum or pins or tacks.

An important rule to follow:
Don't forget to use your brain.

That means leave your plans at home
That qualify as **INSANE!**

NO hanging from the ceiling.

NO flying through the air.

NO swimming in the fish tank.

NO glitter in your hair.

This rule is worth heeding.
It's something I promote.
Don't contradict your teacher.
You will not win her vote.

If she says, "Time to stand."
Don't decide to sit.
If she says, "Time to work."
Don't decide to quit.

If she says, "Get in line."
Do not run about.
And don't forget to raise your hand . . .
Unless you like time-out!

toot
toot

Rule 5:
When in doubt,
DON'T!

This next rule is a **big one**.
It covers things to never do.
The list is rather lengthy,
So sit tight until I'm through.

- Don't growl or hiss or snort.
- Don't thump or bang or spit.
- Don't whistle, burp, or bite.
- Don't whine or kick or hit.
- Don't mimic and don't copy.
- Don't ever, ever swear.
- Don't talk in annoying voices.
- Don't sing too loud or stare.
- Don't act like an animal.
- Don't baa or moo or roar.
- Don't cackle, crow, or bark.
- Don't slither on the floor.

These things are all OFF-LIMITS.
Pay attention to this list!
I, Percy Isaac Gifford, promise there is
nothing that I've missed.
Signed, Percy

Another rule to abide by
(And from this, I never sway):
Do **NOT** take forever
If you've got something to say.

Rule 6:
Make a
long story
short.

If you went to the market,
Don't share every small detail.
Remember: When telling a story,
Just quickly tell your tale.

Though some might disagree,
I think it's **OK** to cry.
But you shouldn't do it often,
And you need a reason why.

If you didn't step in paint,
There's no gum in your hair,
You didn't swallow a pencil
Or glue yourself to a chair,
Then no need for tears and tissues.
Do **NOT** pitch a fit.
Don't act like the world is ending.
Teachers don't like this one bit!

Rule 7.
Don't cry over
spilt milk.

This rule I call the **Golden One**.
There's more you shouldn't do.
I'm talking about stuff to others
That you don't want done to you.

No teasing, taunting, fighting.
No punches, pokes, or kicks.
You should **not** laugh at others.
Never, ever play mean tricks.

The advice I'm about to give you
Isn't hard to comprehend.
It's about how you should act
When the bell rings at day's end.

Don't pull out your pom-poms
Or shout out, "School's a bore!"
Don't lead a chorus of "Hallelujah!"
Don't race out the door.

There's no need to jump for joy
Or trample others as you go.
You're coming back tomorrow.
That's an important thing to know!

I think that covers everything.
Now you know what **NOT** to do.
Just follow my simple rules,
And an **A+** waits for you.

BUT WAIT! There's one more thing.
Another rule that you should know.
It's of critical importance
Before it's off to school you go.

I can't believe I failed to tell you.
And to think we were almost done.
My last and most important rule...

DATE DUE

GAYLORD			PRINTED IN U.S.A.